THE GHOST
AND
MS COX

Also by Alexandria Blaelock

FICTION
That Love Nonsense
Taipan vs Brown

SHORT STORY COLLECTIONS
The Haunting of Hayward Hall
Lovelorn, Lovestruck and Love at First Sight
Common or Garden Variety Heroes
Case Files of the Wilkinson National Detective Agency
Unavoidable Fates
Christmas Travesties
Five Faces of Felicia Clarke
Little Place Called Home

MS BLAELOCK'S BOOKS
Stress Free Dinner Parties
Signature Wardrobe Planning
Holistic Personal Finance
Minimally Viable Housekeeping
Planning a Life Worth Living

SELECTED SHORT STORIES
Alma's Grace
Balancing the Book
Bygone Boyfriend
Christmas Bonanza
Fate in Your Hands
Kiss of Death
Lady of the Looking Glass
Love in the Security Directorate
Morning Star, Evening Star, Superstar
Needy Bitch
Payton's Run
Secret Singer
Shining Star
Ship in a Bottle
The Shadow Thieves
The Palace Hotel
The Pseudonym's Bride

THE GHOST AND MS COX

A SHORT NOVEL

ALEXANDRIA BLAELOCK

BlueMere Books
MELBOURNE, AUSTRALIA

For permission requests, please contact enquiries@bluemerebooks.com.

Ordering Information:
Discounts are available on quantity purchases. For details, contact orders@bluemerebooks.com.

The Ghost and Ms Cox/Alexandria Blaelock
hardback ISBN: 978-1-922744-40-1
paperback ISBN: 978-1-922744-41-8
digital ISBN: 978-1-922744-42-5
AI generated audio: 978-1-922744-50-0

Book Layout © BookDesignTemplates.com
Cover Art © grandfailure/Depositphotos

BlueMere Books
www.bluemerebooks.com

Lest we forget

War does not determine who is right - only who is left.

— BERTRAND RUSSELL

1

To say the letter was a surprise was an understatement.

It arrived addressed to Miss Finlay Cox, which made the contents even more extraordinary.

Finn took it into her barely furnished share house bedroom to open in private.

Before taking off her shoes and changing her clothes.

The letter, from a Melissa Petersen on behalf of Petersen Partners, explained they acted on behalf of the Estate of the Late James Arthur Webb, who died on 25th October 2015.

Finn sat abruptly on the bed, salvaged from a kerbside collection, trying to recollect whether she knew anyone called James Webb.

Certainly no one in her current circle, though someone forgotten from her childhood was always possible.

The letter included a Will, dated 17 July 2009.

The Will stated her name in full as Finlay Margaret Cox, and did not contain any rubbish about dependants or descendants, giving her the impression she was the sole beneficiary...

> *SUBJECT to the payment of my just debts funeral and testamentary expenses I DEVISE and BEQUEATH the residue of my real and personal estate of whatsoever kind and wheresoever situate upon trust to sell, call in, collect and convert into money such parts thereof as shall not consist of money and to distribute the net proceeds of such calling in and conversion (after payment of my just debts funeral and testamentary expenses) to my Trustee UPON TRUST to my sole heir Finlay Margaret Cox.*

The letter instructed her to send her bank account details and verification of her identity.

As far as Finn knew, she'd no family; her mother got pregnant in high school, and her family threw her out.

The sperm donor abandoned them, too.

Her mother'd worked three jobs to keep them housed and fed, and when she died, ridiculously young, Finn went into the foster system.

Shot right out again on her eighteenth birthday when the benefits stopped.

Logically, given she was eight years old at the time, the Victorian Child Protection Service must have approached someone(s) to take custody of her.

Not her father. Her birth certificate listed him as unknown, but her mother's relatives.

It seemed futile to claim her now they were dead too.

So, after the initial shock, when rationality returned, she concluded email spammers had run out of "short cons," and were running "long con" snail-mail scams.

She tucked the letter back into the envelope, threw it on her wonky third-hand flat pack chest of drawers, where subsequent junk soon buried it. Lying forgotten until the next letter arrived about a month later.

It suggested she may not have received the first letter and enclosed a second copy of the will.

Finn thought perhaps this time she ought to do some research, not just dismiss it out of hand.

The Australian Security and Investments Commission listed Petersen Partners as a registered company under the name of Melissa Jane Petersen.

Which seemed legit and warranted further information.

An internet search revealed a website; the phone number on the site was the same as the phone book and the letter. The listed addresses were the same as the ASIC site.

Their registration with the Victorian Legal Services Board and Commissioner was probably more important.

The domiciled town was a couple of hours' drive from Melbourne, which ruled out calling past.

The next day at work, she shut herself in a small, private conversational room, despite being a temp and not technically permitted, to call the number on the letter.

"Hello, Petersen and Partners, Melissa Petersen speaking," she sounded as though she'd run for the phone.

"Oh, hi, it's Finn Cox, calling about the James Webb estate."

"Ah, Finn... Can you hold for a minute while I find the file?"

"Sure."

The phone went silent.

She was just starting to think the woman'd hung up on her when she was back on the line.

"Ah yes, we just need the usual one hundred points of identification, so passport or birth certificate and driver's license is fine. If you could fax or email them?"

"Ah sure. But, are you sure you've the right Finn Cox? I mean, I don't know anyone who'd leave me anything in a Will."

"Quite sure. James is... was your Great Uncle. It took us quite a while to find you."

"I see. At least I think I see."

"Yes, it was difficult. We had to hire a private investigator. You'll send your identification?"

"Um, sure. But can you tell me more about the..." she checked non-specific wording of the Will, "real and personal estate we're talking about?"

"Obviously I can't say much without verifying your identity, but there's a small cottage, some jewellery and some cash."

Finn gasped, "a house?"

"Yes, once we've confirmed your identification, you can have the address."

"And you're sure it's me."

"I'm quite sure, but I need the identification to show due diligence."

More or less confident it wasn't a con, Finn agreed to send her identification.

few Saturdays later, Finn was on her way to inspect the cottage. Her plan was to salvage what she could and put the property on the market. So, she'd plotted a course which made a nice drive in the country.

Planning a pleasant country drive, she'd plotted a course taking in a few small towns along the way; shopping at antique stores and buying fresh farm gate produce.

Hopefully arriving at the cottage late afternoon. Staying overnight, returning in the morning.

Mainly because she couldn't trust her roommates not to break into her padlocked bedroom and nick anything worth taking.

Driving along a winding country road, meandering up and down, around and through the hills, with the windows rolled down, enjoying the last of the summer sunshine.

Through a commemorative Avenue of Honour, planted at the end of the First World War. Predominantly oak trees, the leaves turning red, yellow and brown, falling across the road in a gentle shower.

According to the tourist guide, the community planted each tree in the memory of a local person, but the speed limit was one hundred kilometres per hour, so she was driving too fast to read the tiny name plates at the foot of the trees.

Finn leaned into a curve in the road, noticing the cottage silhouetted against the sunset on the crest of a hill in front of her. Through another bend, it was gone, leaving her with a strange feeling of melancholy.

The road cut through a gully, and as it turned again, there was the cottage again.

Constructed from weatherboards, or maybe raw cedar planks, the walls, along with the tin roof, weathered to an indeterminate grey. The roof streaked with rust.

The type of unloved house that gets a reputation, remembered forever as the haunted house on the hill.

From her vantage point, it looked like a four-room cottage, though the roof line was high, so possibly an attic too. Similar to the dilapidated, almost-forgotten house she'd lived in before her mother died.

The chimney looked to be in the middle of the cottage, so she extrapolated a reception room and bedroom at the front, with a combined kitchen dining room and a second bedroom at the back.

Feeling a wave of nostalgia for a simpler time. Not so much for her own childhood, as for a time when she wasn't responsible for all the decisions she made.

As a kid, she'd hated being told what to do. But now, stuck in a rut, someone telling her what to do seemed a better option.

Stuck in her memories, she overshot the turn, driving a few kilometres further before she found a place safe enough to turn around and come back.

Finn turned into the drive and drove slowly along the gravel, careful to avoid the clay edges where she might get bogged.

The overgrown was mainly a meadow of dandelions surrounding an old oak tree. Perhaps planted after the war to commemorate someone's bright young man.

She pulled up outside the cottage, and having driven for several hours, took a moment to stretch out her back and neck.

Taking a deep eucalyptus-scented breath tinged with the last of the overblown roses and blurring her vision, trying to imagine what the cottage looked like new.

Leaving her bags in the car, she locked it and walked across to the solid looking front door.

She'd expected the house to smell musty or mouldy. Of faded musky perfume and cat pee, but when she opened the door, there was nothing to smell.

Perhaps Melissa Petersen had spoken literally about leaving the door open.

Finn'd been concerned, but the lawyer'd laughed. "It's on a minor road between neighbouring towns. Too far from both for teenaged parties, and far enough from the C road to prevent blow-ins. No one's going to wander into it."

The cottage had been unoccupied for decades, receiving just enough maintenance to keep it standing, so it probably *had* become the local haunted house.

Surprising they hadn't sold it and created a trust with the balance. But, in a small country town, perhaps the firm knew what James wanted, not what he'd said. Or maybe the local market just wasn't that buoyant.

The door opened into a hallway running through the cottage to the back door.

The floorboards seemed straight and true, and the hall stand next to the front door was more or less level across the top, with an old man's hat still hanging from a hook.

The door on her left led to a reception room, kitted out as a reasonably comfortable lounge room. The door on her right opened into a bedroom. Probably the Master.

The second room on the right was a small bedroom, and the door on the left opened into the kitchen.

A lean-to, with a small amount of wood inside, was through the back door on the left; she smiled at the small-ish tin bath hanging from a nail on the wall.

To the right, a water tank sat on a concrete plinth. She tapped it with a knuckle, and it boomed like a drum. Still collecting, probably not leaking.

The remains of a wooden outhouse, overcome by some kind of fruit tree growing up from within it, was situated a little further from the back door.

Now, the cottage and almost ten acres of land were hers. It was beautiful, but she didn't know which part of what she saw was hers.

Her intention to sell almost wavered.

Dusk was drawing in, and with Daylight Savings ending a few weeks before, it was looking like she'd spent too much time dawdling along the way.

Despite the house appearing sound, she'd been mistaken about its habitability - it needed a lot of work to get it up to modern standards.

Creepiness aside, without a functioning bathroom, running water, or electricity, she couldn't really live in it.

And wasn't really keen on staying there overnight either.

Finn pulled her phone from her pocket to check where the closest hotel was, but there was no reception.

Picking the keys up from the kitchen table, she locked the cottage doors and walked back to her car.

Feeling slightly annoyed with herself, she tossed a coin - drive back to the last town or forward to see what was there?

Though, as it turned out, the decision to go forward was a moot point.

When she turned the key, the car didn't start.

The engine clicked, but didn't turn over, as if the battery had died. Stupidly, she clicked it again and again.

The day had been warmish with clear skies, but the temperature had plummeted while she was inside the house.

Without air conditioning, the car was frigid, and would only get colder.

She checked her phone; sixty-three percent charged.

Probably not enough to use as a torch walking down the highway until she found somewhere with better reception.

No idea what was wrong with the car, and turning the key wasn't helping, so she'd no choice but to stay in the cottage.

Eerie as it was, it boasted a wood stove in the kitchen and a hearth in the lounge. Once the stove caught light, she could shut herself in the kitchen to stay warm.

With the light dying, she didn't want to waste the phone battery using it as a torch, so she grabbed her shopping and returned to the kitchen.

If the calendar was anything to go by, nothing had changed since September 1914.

The owner had sandwiched a set of handmade wooden cupboards, topped by the skeleton of a plant, between an icebox and a sink. Nothing in the icebox, thankfully.

The wood stove snuggled into the old hearth with an old box of matches sitting in a tarnished brass dish in a niche carved out of the brick.

Someone had left a teapot with two clean cups and saucers on a tray sitting on the kitchen table, made of the same wood as the cupboards.

Overall, the room looked as though the owners had just popped out for milk, expecting to be back momentarily.

Ms Petersen would've made an excellent real estate agent.

After a second trip to the car to retrieve her hand and overnight bag, she hesitated at the front door, key in hand.

Her first instinct was to lock herself inside, but, given the whole weird house thing, would she need a quick getaway to run down the drive screaming?

She reminded herself she didn't believe in ghosts, but believed in rapists and murderers.

She locked the door and retreated to the kitchen.

First, she lit a lavender-scented hand-poured beeswax candle, then she used it to rifle through the cupboards to find a plate to put it on.

The next concern was bringing some wood in before full dark so, she picked up a metal bucket presumably used for that purpose.

Having stacked some wood in it, hopefully sans spiders, and getting two splinters on the way, she lugged it back inside.

Opening the stove's small door, she found a fire already laid.

She grinned. Melissa Petersen hadn't spared any effort.

It looked ready to go, so crossing her fingers she lit it - better to find out whether it worked now, and whether she could keep the fire going later.

It lit well enough, and the fire caught hold, so she dared to close the door and experiment with the flue until she thought she understood it. She didn't know how long the wood would last, but hopefully, the night at least.

Luckily Finn hadn't got around to moving the ten-litre bottle of water from the boot and into her room, so she set it next to the sink and gave her hands a quick wash.

And discovered the sink was the old-fashioned kind that empties into a bucket you carry out to the outhouse a couple of times a day.

Cursing, she went back outside for the bath, put the wood in it, and the bucket back under the sink.

Next, she found a corkscrew and a glass, rinsed it with some bottled water (because she didn't think anyone had washed it since 1914), and poured herself some Cabernet Sauvignon. Almost to the top.

She took a sip, held the wine in her mouth for a moment, and then swallowed. As the wine settled in her stomach, she relaxed.

Or at the very least, not worry so much about what lurked in the shadows.

Exhausted, she yawned, pulled her chair up to the fire, and took another sip of wine.

The cottage was more or less silent, but the sound of the night was almost musical as the magpies tried to out sing the kookaburras. A light wind blew through the oak tree and brushed the bushes along the side of the cottage. The weather boards creaked as they tensed with the cold, and the fire crackled.

Homely. Comforting. Reminiscent.

And then she remembered she didn't live there.

Neither was she really interested in staying there.

The logical thing to do was to sell the property, and use it as a deposit for a tiny one-bedroom flat in the City.

One she could have all to herself.

She'd mainly visited out of curiosity. To see if she felt some kind of connection to the place.

The fire warmed up the kitchen, helping to chase away the shadows.

There was nothing to do, nowhere to go, and she wasn't entirely sure what to do with herself.

The warmth, wine and silence were making her drowsy until something with four legs thudded across the tin roof, startling her awake with a pounding heart.

Finn took another sip of wine and trying not to creep herself out by thinking too much about the house or what the creature was.

To distract herself, she opened a paper bag of seeded crackers, and the paper-wrapped artisan Brie to go with it. Then opened all the drawers to find a knife and scrape some cheese onto a cracker.

With the Brie, the venison and Armagnac pate, pickles and sliced meats, it was a nice, if snackish meal.

What she needed was something to listen to, to take her mind off everything else, and the latest episode of the True Crime podcast she'd been listening to would do just that.

She reached for her phone, opened up the podcast app, and listened through the speakers rather than her earbuds for a while as she ate.

And realised, perhaps the grisly murder of a woman on her own probably wasn't the best thing to be listening to when she was alone in a creepy old house in the middle of nowhere.

She thought she heard someone skipping down the stairs, jaunty steps like you'd make when you've got something fun planned.

And half-expected one of her share house "friends" to walk through the kitchen door.

Before remembering, she wasn't at home.

Was wide awake, despite not believing in ghosts.

She remembered seeing a clock on the fireplace mantle in the reception room.

If she wound it up, it might distract her from the other noises. At the worse, it would give her something to listen to as it counted the seconds of her life down.

After a moment of summoning her courage, she walked back to the reception room.

The room was chilly. The boards creaked as she crossed the threshold, and she couldn't stop herself from looking back.

Of course, there was no one there.

She shuddered extravagantly, picked the clock off the mantelpiece and, cradling it to her chest, ran back to the kitchen. The key was still in the back and turned smoothly as she wound up the mechanism.

When the key stopped winding, she wound the hands forward, jumping when it chimed the first time.

It seemed to take forever to figure out where the switch was to turn it off. And then she wound the hands forward to the correct time.

The regular tick was soothing as she laid her arm on the table, and her head on her arm, to watch the clock, listening to the movement of its second hand.

It was beautiful. Dark wood with a mounded dome supported by four ivory columns; the once white face sporting large black numbers. She thought she might take it home.

Finn closed her eyes to better imagine where it might go and gently fell asleep.

3

Finn dreamt a young man's jaunty footsteps skipped down the stairs.

A tall and straight young man with dark hair, and the whisper of a moustache. With the kind of muscles developed by working hard on the land; chopping wood, planting crops, mustering cattle.

Wearing a new Light Horse Regimental uniform.

With her knowledge of the Light Horse campaigns, her heart bled for him and his doomed youth as he swaggered around the kitchen.

Chances were, he'd been blown to bits rather than dying at home in his sleep.

From the top of his new, unstained and still rigid emu feather decorated hat, to his puttee clad legs and boots, he was the epitome of youth and excitement.

"Well Finny, what do you think?" he asked, turning, striking a pose and turning again.

"Ah, it looks quite dashing on you."

"It is rather, isn't it?"

He flung himself onto a kitchen chair, leaning across the table to take her folded hands. "You will wait for me, won't you?"

"Of course. You'll be back here lickedy-split," she attempted to smile at him with suddenly dry lips.

"They say it will be over by Christmas, but I hope there'll be plenty of Hun left for me when I get there."

"Don't say that! The war will change you. You won't be the same man when you come back. Assuming you even get back."

He leant across the table and gifted her a kiss, "don't be silly, I'm doing it for you, to keep you safe!"

Finn frowned and thought of Horace and Wilfred Owen. Dulce et decorum est pro patria mori - how sweet and fitting to die for the homeland.

Though maybe those who died were better off than those who came back.

She opened her mouth to protest, but chances are he wouldn't believe her, so there wasn't much point in saying anything further.

This young man was full of a young man's confidence.

He'd never dealt with difficult circumstances; probably couldn't imagine a situation he couldn't deal with.

He certainly didn't understand the toll those experiences would take on those who came back.

A lifetime of post-traumatic stress and drunkenness if he was lucky, maimed or horribly disfigured at worse.

All those young men.

It was a tragedy.

Especially the reckless boys who added four or five years to their age, and all those stupid recruitment officers who winked and let them go. Those poor boys who died before they'd even lived.

The lost generation; you'd think we'd have learned something by now.

Finn didn't want this man, whoever he was, to die without experiencing some of what life offered, so she kissed him and took his hand, leading him back to the front of the cottage and into the bedroom.

"Are you sure about this, Finny?"

"I've never been as sure about anything in my life," she replied as she sat on his bed and kissed him again.

4

The sun streaming through the window woke Finn. Gently surfacing from sleep, listening to kookaburras laugh, and enjoying the sensation of being warm and snug in bed.

Aside from the birds, all was quiet and still, nothing to ruin the day.

Yet.

Eyes still closed, Finn enjoyed the moment for a few minutes more, and stretched. Luxuriating in the afterglow.

And paused mid-stretch, realised something wasn't right.

She didn't generally hear kookaburras in her Richmond share house, and her room didn't catch the morning sun.

After another moment, she remembered the long drive out to the cottage.

And falling asleep in the kitchen, then bolted upright.

She was naked, with her clothes strewn around the bed.

Exactly as she'd expect had she brought a boy home on a Friday night.

But so far as she knew, she'd fallen asleep fully dressed, resting her head on the kitchen table.

She listened carefully and couldn't hear any sound of human activity.

Also, exactly as she'd expect given most Friday night boys would be long by now.

But, again, she'd fallen asleep fully dressed, resting her head on the kitchen table, so who'd she had sex with last night?

Her thoughts turned back to rapists and murderers, but she knew she'd locked the door, so how did they get in?

She hopped around the room, grabbing her clothes and trying to get them on quietly, then ducked back to the kitchen.

The kitchen looked the same as she'd left it - shopping bags, empty wine bottle, the wreckage of cheese and crackers.

Except the stove, strangely, hadn't gone out overnight. Which she was pretty sure wasn't anything to do with her.

Though she couldn't help but appreciate the stove put out a great deal of heat.

Or was it a thin layer of nervous energy overlaying sheer panic keeping her warm?

She checked the front and back doors were both locked, and at a glance, it seemed the windows were still closed too.

Panic receded.

It was a long time since she'd had sex. Was it possible abstinence caused the vivid dream?

So vivid she'd those odd little muscle aches you got after a good night?

It was the only explanation she was prepared to acknowledge.

But now there was a problem of the bathroom variety, and the only way to deal with it was to find a bush out of view of the road and the drive.

She took her purse pack of tissues.

The less said about that, the better.

What she really needed was coffee.

She thought she'd seen a stovetop percolator in her rifle through the cupboards, so she fished it out, rinsed it and scooped in some of the blend she'd bought.

Just the smell of it made her feel better.

Life always seems more manageable when you've had coffee, and even though it was an espresso with no milk or sugar, that morning was no exception.

In fact, she felt cheerful enough to sit on the back porch step, looking out over the property.

Appreciating the silence and sense of spaciousness.

And her land - the orchard of goodness knows what old fruit trees, the paddock for a horse, maybe.

And the water tanks looked to be a good size, probably more than enough for one person's needs.

Having spent the night there, a sense of ownership crept over her.

Could she live in this little house?

Melbourne was busy. And the Richmond house she lived in was never quiet. Much as she liked her roommates individually, they were always coming and going at odd hours with strangers.

But could she survive alone with all this space and silence around her?

She'd need an income; she couldn't commute two hours to and from Melbourne every day.

In any case, temping through eight agencies was a bit of a drag when the jobs ran out, but if there was an agency in a town nearby, she could register there.

Then again, over the years, she'd gained enough assorted skills she could perhaps set up as some kind of freelancer.

But she'd need the internet, and the internet needed power.

On the plus side, if she lived and worked from the cottage, she'd save herself almost two thousand dollars a month with next to no costs.

How long would it take to get a vegetable garden going?

She thought she saw something out of the corner of her eye and turned her head a fraction to see.

And for a moment, she thought she saw the guy from her dream looking at her wistfully.

She shook her head, and then her body.

Must be delusional.

She went back into the house to drop off her cup and bring her phone back outside to check the reception, and this time she got a bar.

Not enough to do anything with, but a positive sign nonetheless.

In a spurt of optimism, she went back through the house for her car keys and out to see if the car worked, and this time, the engine caught immediately.

Odd, but maybe all it needed was a quiet night in.

On her way back into the house, she glanced into the reception room and saw a photo of a young man in uniform. She backtracked to look at it more closely.

It could've been her dream boy. They looked about the same age, but there was something a little more desperate about the dream boy.

There'd been a small table with a framed photo next to the bed, but she hadn't looked at the picture.

She took the lounge room picture to the bedroom to compare them.

As she crossed the threshold, she felt a chill and clutched her jacket around her.

Someone walking over her grave?

Finn saw something move out of the corner of her eye and whipped around, but it was only her reflection in a spotted mirror on the wardrobe door. It hung open, clothes spilling out.

Shutting the door, she moved across to the photo.

It was a young woman in a long-sleeved stripy dress with a nipped-in waist and a scallop decoration around the hem. An enormous hat on her blond hair, and a rather large ring on her left ring finger. Some kind of square dark stone with the suggestion of a larger setting.

Finn sat on the bed and held the two pictures up together. They suited each other.

Though who were they? She guessed one or both of them were related to her, but how?

And what else might she find in the way of personal papers if she rifled through all the cupboards and drawers?

If she did it now, she could still get back to Melbourne before dusk.

"Please forgive me," she said out loud and started looking for papers.

It took a couple of drawers, but it was apparent this was a man's room.

No women's clothing and no feminine touches.

She collected together some books and papers, taking it all into the lounge. Then rifled through the sideboard and bookshelf, collecting a few more papers, a couple of books, and a few more photos.

Back in the kitchen, she emptied one of her shopping bags into the other and put the collection in it before checking the second bedroom.

Nothing obviously worth taking; though it was more of a storage space than a sleep space, and she didn't really want to give it the time it deserved.

Then she collected everything together and loaded the car.

Took one last walk through the rooms to make sure she hadn't forgotten anything, but partly because she didn't really want to leave.

With nothing but trees and wheat fields around her, the space and silence were restorative.

Or maybe it was the vivid dream...

She made sure the windows were closed and the doors locked, then left the cottage behind her.

As she looked back at the cottage in the rear-view mirror, she thought for a moment she saw a man slouching in the bedroom window.

5

Back in Melbourne, she found her usual routine strangely constrictive.

She caught a jam-packed train two stations to get to the city early enough to be "on-call" with one of her agencies in return for free breakfast, walking home through teeming streets.

No matter the day or time she visited the supermarket, it was stuffed with shoppers.

Everywhere she went there was noise and people; many of them smelling less than fresh.

And as she "relaxed" at home, trying to get a grip on the papers she'd brought back with her, she found the smell of Chinese and Indian takeout nauseating, when she hadn't previously noticed it at all.

One of her roommates moved out, and some younger, night owl student moved in and jacked up the sound system at midnight.

And much as she tried to recapture that dream, it receded from her almost faster than the days went by; every potential physical replacement she met wasn't worth looking at once, let alone twice.

No matter how much she drank.

She looked into how much it might cost to get the electricity connected, and whether solar panels were a viable alternative.

And if there were mains, water or gas pipes nearby. Then how much propane deliveries would cost.

Followed by how to filter and treat the water tanks so she could safely drink the water inside them.

And what the planning requirements might be to get the upgrades done.

6

About a week later, Melissa Petersen called.

"Just checking in to see what you thought about the cottage?"

"I like it, but there's a lot of work that needs doing if I'm going to move in."

"So you're interested in keeping the place? I thought you'd be of a mind to sell it."

"I am. But it'd be foolish to sell without thinking about what it'd take to get it up and running. And whether I could live there on my own, so far from anyone else."

"Well, it's less than half an hour from the towns that surround it, and these days that's not far at all."

"True. In the city it sometimes takes me half an hour to drive some place I could walk in ten minutes."

"Could you work remotely?"

"No. Yes. I'd probably have to work out my current contract, but I guess I could start up an online business to keep me going."

"Or you could do some work for me - I've got a backlog of stuff that needs doing, and once word gets around, you'll find there are a few people in town who need a hand with once-of jobs."

"I'm really tempted, but I think I'd need to stay for a week or so to get a feel for it."

"Like camping!"

"Just like camping," Finn agreed.

7

When Finn arrived at the cottage mid-afternoon Saturday, it was almost exactly as she remembered it.

As she pulled into the drive, she felt strangely lighter, more relaxed, the feeling you get when you know you're home.

She brought her bags and boxes inside and stacked them up in the kitchen.

Blessing Melissa when she saw the empty sink bucket and the fire'd been re-laid. She lit it, rubbing her hands and holding them out for warmth.

It felt like Melissa was encouraging her to move; though she probably just wanted to complete the paperwork.

Finn took a small shovel outside and dug herself a temporary toilet for the duration, leaving the soil piled up beside it, ready to cover her deposits.

She was nervous about this aspect of the week, but she reassured herself she'd been camping in an actual tent before, and an actual cottage with heating was so much better than a tent.

Though of course, the thing that made doing your business in the great outdoors bearable was the prospect of going home to do it indoors.

Plus, she could always drive to one of the towns to a café or pub for a meal, and take care of "the business" while she was there.

Not that going elsewhere was a viable option.

She poured some tank water into the big buckets she'd brought and dropped some water purifying tablets in. There was also a filter jug to further treat the water before she drank it.

Just in case.

Maybe over the top, but the last thing she needed was to get sick, in the middle of nowhere, with no mobile reception.

Her other purchases included power banks, torches and a battery-powered radio.

As far as Finn could tell, everything she could conceivably need was in the cottage with her. Even if she'd spent too much money on too much stuff for one week.

Still cost less than a week in the closest hotel.

Not to mention she could use some of it in her everyday life.

And she'd bought most of it on sale.

And, well, she needed it to stay in the cottage, and that was really all that mattered.

She unpacked, storing her supplies in the icebox, and putting a small battery-powered cooler fridge on top of it.

After that extraordinarily vivid dream, Finn hesitated at the door to the Master bedroom, clutching a blow-up mattress and sleeping bag to her chest.

The hair stood up on her skin, and she wasn't sure whether to even open the door, let alone sleep in there.

Someone had made the bed, with the patchwork quilt on the top, leaving no sign she'd ever been there.

Thanks again Melissa.

Her cheeks grew warm as she remembered what'd happened in the room.

But.

If this was her house, and it was, then this was her bedroom.

Though should she choose to keep the cottage, she'd definitely need a new mattress. Maybe even a new bed.

Who was she kidding? She'd seventy-five percent decided already.

Resolutely, she rolled out the self-inflating mattress on the floor, topped it with the sleeping bag, opened the valves, and left the mattress to inflate.

Bed made!

With the cell phone reception dodgy, to put it politely, she'd need a reliable clock, and as it wasn't still in the kitchen, went to the lounge to collect it.

Aside from the picture she'd removed, it was exactly the same, the clock back on the mantlepiece.

She wound it up and set it to the right time.

It was still light outside, so she went for a walk to survey her property. Still a little uncertain about her ability to live by herself miles from anywhere.

Though, to be honest, she was always lonely, regardless of how many people were with her. Being lonely while alone might be a refreshing change.

Obviously, someone'd once lived here, perhaps her soldier. Or as she now knew him, Archie Webb.

It wasn't clear to her whether he'd bought the place, or inherited it. His name was the first on the title, but his family could just as easily hived a parcel off their own land for him.

There wasn't a genuine need to make an urgent decision about the cottage; she could get the title transferred to her and worry about the rest later.

Though there was a tax benefit to selling it with the proceeds going to James' Estate, rather than to her, but it was hard to decide either way.

She sighed and turned to look at the cottage. It was sweet or *would* eventually be sweet. Unlike the Richmond house, which would be nothing more than ugly. Or surrounded by miles and miles of people-free space.

There her bedroom had a view of someone's wall, here a view without buildings.

The streets were never silent back there, but the cottage was full of the sounds of nature; wind in the trees, birdsong, insects.

It made her want to relax and take her time.

Keep it simple, sweetie.

There was plenty of roof space to install solar panels, and probably enough for a small wind turbine to supplement the panels.

The eaves and walls were sufficiently wide to store the batteries. And a water filtration system, which she now knew she could plumb into the house.

She had some savings, but would there be enough with the bequest to fund all the work?

Giving herself a good shake, she ladled some water from the buckets into the jugs and took them back inside to get something to eat.

She wasn't hungry as such, but the evening was drawing in, and eating gave her something to do while she waited for bedtime.

She changed out of her jeans, and into her track pants, fleece top, and ugg boots, nervous and excited about what the night might bring.

Another vivid dream?

Or perhaps nothing.

After her meal, she took a candle into the lounge and lit the fire already laid in the hearth. She could have taken a torch, but somehow candlelight seemed more suitable.

When she was sure the fire was properly lit, she collected her laptop, a pillow, and blanket into the lounge.

Snuggling into the couch, Finn rested her feet on the coffee table, pulling the blanket up around her legs and chest, and drew the laptop into her lap.

She'd downloaded a few detective shows to an external drive, and once she was comfortable, started playing the first.

When the first episode finished, the second started playing.

Finn noticed a chill in the air and snuggled a little deeper into her blanket.

From the corner of her eye, she saw her soldier sitting next to her; a little fuzzy around the edges. Her brain and body seized up; she couldn't think of anything sensible to do, (aside from run away screaming), but couldn't set her muscles into action.

<Not a soldier,> the voice appeared in her head, <Archie>.

Archie, she thought.

Wondering if falling asleep explained why she couldn't move.

Asleep, dreaming, not waking up.

Any time now, she'd wake up.

But she didn't.

<What is this thing, this stage show in a box?> the thought came.

Surprise trumping shock, Finn turned her head to look at him. He might have been more than a century old...

Or a century dead, but still just a boy. A naïve, innocent farm boy at that.

A cute, naïve, innocent farm boy.

And aside from the horror of war, a boy with the equivalent life experience of the average modern ten-year-old.

And ghost or not, it was hard to be afraid of someone so childlike.

She faced forward again, trying not to notice she could see through him.

"It's exactly that, a recording of a stage play in a special box."

<Is it not perhaps a little graphic for ladies?>

She snorted, "not these days. After two world wars, women don't really have the option of being delicate anymore."

<Two world wars? Did I die for nothing?">

"Ummm. No, not really. Australia has never been conquered."

<Well, that's a relief.>

"Yeah, but we're controlled by international conglomerations instead."

<I don't understand.>

"Well, let's just focus on the positives, shall we? We were on the winning side of both of them. And all the little ones that followed. You and your regiment are legendary heroes, one and all."

<The War to end all Wars?>

"That's the one."

Archie went quiet, but remained next to her, as the episode ended, and the laptop scrolled onto the next one.

But somewhere during the following forty-five minutes, he disappeared, and she found herself worried about him.

Though really, what was the point of worrying about a dead boy? It wasn't like anything worse could happen to him, was it?

She tried to imagine how she'd feel if she, well, not died, but something like going to prison for a couple of decades.

For some kind of peaceful protest, convinced she'd made a difference. Only to be let out again to find everything was worse.

Had he been "alive" and waiting since he died?

But waiting for what? Or who?

His girlfriend, who must surely have moved on and married someone else?

Or moved to Melbourne and got an education like so many other single women did at the time.

The rest of his regiment? Waiting to form a ghost unit marching to the hereafter?

James, his brother, who'd left her this cottage?

Though the dates didn't really add up; James can't have been born before Archie went away. Maybe not even before he'd died.

Finn shook her head and shut the laptop, not interested in murder mysteries anymore.

And bedtime brought something else to worry about. Was Archie sulking in the bedroom, and did she have the right to disturb him?

Well, damn it all to hell, it was her house now.

She stood up, squared her shoulders, took the candle, and threw the bedroom door open.

There was no one there, so she crawled into her sleeping bag on the air mattress, blew out the candle and settled down.

She didn't think she'd sleep, but given the wine, the long drive, and the lateness of the night...

8

After a deep, refreshing sleep, Finn woke alone.

Bloody freezing, with an aching back from sleeping on the floor.

Both the fire in the lounge, and the stove in the kitchen had gone out because she'd no idea how to bank them properly to make sure they stayed alive overnight.

The house felt empty.

As empty as if no one ever lived there.

The small sighs and scuffles she made echoed disturbingly in a way she didn't recall them doing before.

As if even the resident ghost had moved out.

Assuming he was a ghost and not the product of her imagination.

Even worse, the house smelled the musty you get when you shut your room up and go away for a week in winter.

Cold, damp, and still.

She shuddered.

What Finn really needed was coffee, but before she could do anything else, an urgent trip behind the bushes was required.

The ground crunched with early frost, and the cold on her bare bottom was almost enough to make her run back inside without taking care of the business.

Bathroom taken care of, she wondered what time on a Sunday, the closest café opened.

Decided she couldn't wait, and retrieving the box with her camping supplies, felt around until she found the sale catalogue with handy camping tips.

Which turned out to be useless, given she wasn't concerned with creepy crawlies, getting the car bogged in clay, or purifying river water.

Would've been better to bring a small liquid gas stove with her.

She got an internet connection with her phone and quickly searched how to lay a fire, then how to bank one.

Once she had a good fire going, she put some of her stored purified water on to boil, and then retrieved another couple of buckets of water from the tank, dropping more purifier tablets in there.

All the while, very conscious of being alone.

As she drank her coffee, she wondered if she'd accidentally performed a do-it-yourself exorcism, and strangely, found the house much less appealing than on the drive up.

The quiet solitude, so beguiling in the Melbourne bustle, was feeling more like sensory deprivation torture.

Finn changed back into her jeans, jumper and boots, grabbed her bag and drove into Melissa Petersen's town.

But not before carefully banking the fire.

She parked the car on the wide main street outside a shop advertising a closing down sale; one that may have occurred a decade or two previously, going by the faded sign.

Shoving her hands in her pockets, she glanced around before mentally tossing a coin and walking to her left.

Depressingly, there were a lot of empty shops, the fittings still inside under a thick layer of dust. Looking a lot like the town centre was dying.

She was a little glad Archie wasn't around to see it, but wondered what he might have thought about it.

A little ahead, a shop window cast a cheery yellow light across the street.

And as Finn got closer, a swell of appropriately Sunday morning orchestral choral music increased in volume.

Nearer the shop, a small room spanning the frontage, with a reception desk on one side, a row of hard wood chairs on the other and a coffee table of magazines a footstep away from the chairs.

Through the door into what she assumed was a book-lined consulting room, she could see a long table surrounded by chairs, part of which was covered with books and papers.

Her footsteps slowed as she glanced up at the sign suspended from the roof. In some kind of old-fashioned print, it announced Petersen Partners.

Melissa's office then.

Was she inside?

Should she knock on the door?

And then a woman behind her took the matter out of her hands, by saying, "we're not open today. Could you come back tomorrow after nine?"

Finn turned around to see almost the opposite of what she'd expected; a tall, thin, young woman with dark hair and green eyes.

"Ah," she said, then took a sip from her steaming vacuum flask. "You'll be Finlay Margaret Cox. How are you?" she held out her hand.

"Please call me Finn," smiling, she pulled an icy hand out of her pocket and clasped Melissa's slightly warmer hand, "how do you know who I am?"

"I've not seen you around here before, and recognise you from your photo identification."

"You must be Melissa Petersen then," Finn said.

The woman grinned, "the one and only, but please call me Mel. Would you like to come inside where it's marginally warmer?"

"Sure."

She waited as the woman unlocked the door and pushed it open.

"Where are the other partners?"

Mel laughed, "it's just me now. The founder was my great-great-great-grandfather, and when his sons joined the business, he made it a partnership."

"Then they must have known the Webbs."

"Like as not. We were the only lawyers in town until after the Second World War."

"Wouldn't have thought they'd have much to do in a small town."

"Wasn't always this small, but a lot of wills, conveyancing, employment contracts."

Mel gestured her through to the big room with the table and pulled out a seat for Finn. "Come inside take a seat. I'll be right back."

"Ah no, I didn't mean to disturb you. I just wanted to thank you for cleaning the cottage again for me."

"Cleaning the cottage? I didn't arrange that. But seeing as you're here, let's go through a few things."

Finn sat at the big table, and looked around her, appreciating the solidity of the mahogany furniture, and its overwhelming sense of history.

Mel came back with a book, a large bulky envelope, a pen and a cup. Setting them on the table, she poured some coffee from her flask into the cup, "milk and two sugars, if that's okay."

"No really, that's okay."

She wrinkled her nose, "then you'll have to wait until lunchtime when the pub opens for your next fix."

"Ah," said Finn and picked up the cup, "cheers," she toasted Mel, who raised her flask back at her.

"The first thing," said Mel, flipping open the book and writing in it, then laying the pen along the gutter, "is to give you the jewellery. If you could sign here to say you've received it," she pointed. Finn signed next to her name as Mel slid the envelope across the table.

"Must be nice to have a sense of history, to know where you came from," Finn said, shoving the envelope into her bag.

Mel made a doubtful noise. "When I was younger and there were more of us, I used to find it oppressive. So many old men who used to be lawyers looking down at me because I was all that was left."

"I had no one else but Mum, and she was so... Angry I suppose, but she never said anything about anyone else. I don't even know how I'm related to James and Archie Webb."

"You didn't say as much on the phone, but I'd the idea that was why you decided to take a vacation here. I don't know anything offhand, but we probably have some records here. And some of it you could get through Births, Deaths and Marriages Victoria. There might even be something in the cottage."

"Thanks for the tips," Finn said, leaning both elbows on the table and cupping her hands around the cup for warmth. "It didn't bother me before, but there's something about this place, and I just can't put a finger on it."

Mel sipped her coffee, quiet for the moment. Appearing to reach a decision, she said, "why don't you come with me and I'll show you about the place?"

Finn roused herself from her gloomy thoughts, "sorry, what?"

Mel laughed, "drink your coffee, we're going on a mini-road trip."

Almost before she'd drunk it, Mel took it away through a door, presumably to a kitchen given she came back without it. Then bustled around, turning off the music and the light switches, and Finn out the door.

"I didn't mean to interrupt your work," Finn said.

"Pfft. It'll still be there, no matter how long I play hooky for. Anyway," she said with a smile, "you said you'd come work for me when you move out here."

Mel set a brisk pace up to her zippy little red car, and Finn squeezed herself in.

First was the cemetery, mostly green grass with hibernating roses bordering the paths. A muddy patch surrounding a tarpaulin suggested an upcoming funeral.

Mel led the way to the eastern corner, and up a grassy slope to an area with low, modest markers.

"This is the Protestant area," she pointed to a marker, "and these are the Webbs. They put the original stone here when James' brother Archie was lost in the First World War. They didn't know where, or if Archie was buried, and realistically, they were never going to go to Turkey or France, so this was a good compromise.

"Their mother died as the Second World War was breaking out. They said it was from a broken heart when James enlisted.

"And this is also where we laid James to rest."

Finn cleared her throat, "I feel like I should say something."

Mel shrugged, "now you know where he is, you can come back and talk in private. So to speak."

They stood in silence for a moment longer, before Mel led the way down and across the cemetery to an area with large marble monuments, statues of angels and largish urns of cut flowers.

"This is the Roman Catholic section where they laid the Coxes to rest. I didn't look into who your parents are, but I expect they'll be around here somewhere."

"I have no idea who my father is, let alone whether he's still alive, and my mum's ashes are in a Milo tin in my wardrobe."

Mel looked horrified, "I don't want to upset you, but that's so disrespectful."

"Ah no, it's not like that! An old roommate broke the urn looking for drugs or money or something in the ashes."

Mel grimaced, "that's so awful I don't know what to say."

Finn smiled grimly, "I scraped her up and put her in the tin. I suppose I should have scattered her ashes like she wanted me to, but I wasn't ready to let her go at that point."

"I understand. I felt so bad about losing my first cat when I was a teenager that I now have a pet columbarium in the back room."

Finn looked at the forest of elaborate monuments surrounding her, "I'm getting a picture of what her family were like. And why she never came back. And maybe I understand a little why she didn't want me having anything to do with them. But it doesn't really explain why they didn't want me."

"I think there are one or two of the Coxes left in the nursing home up in the big town, but they're ancient. You might as well say there's nothing left of them here."

Finn turned her back to look up at the Protestant section with its small neat graves.

"It's ridiculous to think of a man I don't know and never met as more of a family than this lot," she gestured with her thumb at the monuments behind her. "Is it possible my father's family were Webbs?"

"Absolutely. But there aren't any Webbs left here, so we'd have to do some more research.

"Ummm... You could check the local newspaper office archives to see if there's anything there about school dances or whatnot.

"Oh right, the local paper shut down. Did the archives transfer to the library or the historical society? Or maybe the museum. I'll find out."

A gust of wind swirled fallen leaves along the paths and, sighing, Finn looked between the two potential branches of her family, thinking about her mother.

So stubbornly determined to do it on her own.

Without help.

Not even allowing Finn to ask them for help when she got sick.

Then again, maybe her mother'd asked for help and they'd knocked her back.

What kind of people would throw their own daughter out anyway?

And not just their child, but their grandchild as well.

None of it was Finn's fault, but she just couldn't get her head around it.

Finn thought of Archie, alone in the universe, sighing again and turned to Mel, "I thought I'd feel something here among the dead, but there's nothing here."

"Then let's look at some of the living places here in town."

And led her on a tour of the recently closed local high school with the last few pupils being bused to the big town.

The sports centre was still operational, with netball, basketball, and indoor soccer leagues, practice cricket nets, and table tennis.

Mel checked her phone, "pub's open," fancy a drink?"

"I'm sorry. I didn't mean to take up all your time."

"Pfft. All work and no play makes Mel a dull girl. Come on."

Mel drove back to her office, then led Finn across the expanse of road, "camel trains need a large turning circle," she said waving at the road.

"Camel trains?"

"Like stage coaches, only camels. Actually, more like freight trains for wool."

"Huh," Finn said.

Inside, she ordered slow-cooked beef stew and red wine for two. And spent the next couple of hours meeting Mel's friends.

Back at the cottage, Finn nursed the fire back to life, and put the kettle on to boil while she changed back into her track pants and fleece.

Then made a mug of tea and looked out the window as she drank it.

Mel's friends were welcoming, and she thought it might be possible to settle in and build a life.

But she worried moving to a country town might be going overboard.

A throat cleared behind her, and she turned to see Archie. Blurry around the edges, "are you okay?" she asked.

He smiled a half-hearted smile, "I'm not sure. How about you?"

She shrugged her shoulders, "can I get you anything?"

"I'd love a cup of tea."

Not convinced he could drink it, she shrugged and put the kettle on again.

"I feel I owe you an apology," he said.

"Not really. I should apologise to you for dumping all that stuff on you."

"I feel like I died for nothing."

Finn took a sip of tea, "I wouldn't go that far. The Light Horse has come to represent our national character. It was only through your war that we came to understand ourselves as Australians."

"Really?"

"God's own truth."

He nodded, "not as good as saving the world from war, but not bad."

Finn drank some more tea, watching him come a little more into focus, and a little more solid.

The kettle boiled, and Finn made another mug of tea, and very curious about what he'd do with it, put it on the table near him.

He reached for it, but couldn't grasp it.

Finn turned away so she wouldn't see his frustration, and noticed her bag with the envelope of jewellery in it.

She grabbed it out and emptied it out on the table. A couple of small boxes, some loose tangled up strings of beads and chains, and something wrapped in paper.

She opened a box to find a silver-coloured ring with a square emerald surrounded by tiny diamonds, and the other to find a silver locket. She opened it to find pictures of two soldiers, one of them Archie.

"Who's this?" she asked, turning around to show him.

But he was gone.

She couldn't be sure, but she thought the level of the tea in the mug had gone down.

Smiling, she lay the locket down and tried separating the chains.

Which didn't take too long to get annoying, so she turned to the folded-up paper instead.

As she unravelled it, a separate paper-wrapped package fell to the table with a clunk.

The paper in her hand looked to be a letter, two pages, written on both sides in spiky, hard to decipher copperplate handwriting. She flipped to the last page to see it was from James. Then flipped back to the front to look at the date - 9 May 2015, written just a few months before he died.

Curious, she read it first.

She skimmed the first page, then pulled a chair out and sat down.

James was her mother's mother's brother, meaning Archie was her Great Uncle. So, Mel was right; one mystery about her family revealed and confirmed.

She kept reading.

> *I wanted to write you more about where you come from. I'm sure you'll want to know.*
>
> *I've no idea why my sister Edith married Wally (your grandfather). She certainly didn't seem fond of him, even at the beginning. There weren't many that came back from the war, so perhaps she was afraid she wouldn't find anyone else. Not in this small town any rate. And she certainly didn't want to have to stay home to look after our ageing parents.*

It wasn't a happy marriage. Wally was a drinker and got violent. Edith was always trying to hide the bruises, and we were always trying not to notice. I wish I'd said something about them at the time, but they were different times. It was a man's right to discipline his family as he saw fit.

It was many years before she carried a child to term, becoming more bitter, resentful, and angry with each miscarriage. It was hard to see my beautiful sister so unable to let go of any slight, and many of her friends dropped her because they couldn't deal with her scorn. Which made her worse.

A seemingly never-ending spiral down towards depression. Not that we knew it was that at the time, we just thought she was a sourpuss.

Edith was about forty when Kaye was born, and we were so worried about how your mother'd be growing up in that house, but Edith threw her life into her daughter.

Your mother was a happy child, loved everyone and everything. And she was a delight to be around, so everyone loved her. If she noticed any coolness towards her mother, she didn't say anything about it.

The Agricultural Show was the highlight of the year. There were displays of agricultural and household equipment, and new kinds of preserved food and drinks.

And competitions for best livestock, fleece, arts and crafts, food and wine. You might like to know I was the wood chop champion a couple of years running.

We enjoyed our grown-up pursuits while the kids entertained themselves at the carnival.

We'd meet our friends and neighbours for picnic lunches, and a couple of beers, and at the end of the day, take everyone home again. They were good times.

The point is that we are a townie family, but there are also carnie families. Every year, the same families returning year after year, in a way, Kaye grew up with them too.

The carnies loved your mother too, especially the Wiltshaws, and their son Tom. Whenever they were in town, Tom and Kaye were inseparable.

By the time she found out she was pregnant, they'd moved on. And in those days, we didn't know how to find them. Maybe you can find him now.

Wally was livid and kicked her out. She stayed with me for a bit while Edith pleaded with Wally to change his mind. But he was a stubborn old coot who never changed his mind and he beat Edith black and blue for suggesting it. To punish the both of them, I suppose.

Kaye felt like she had no choice but to leave town, so he didn't beat her mother to death. It was a lot for her to take on, but she was stubborn as well in her own way.

Edith was heartbroken, and it killed her. She didn't even live out the year.

Wally blamed Kaye, but when he himself was dying, he wanted to see her one last time, but she refused. Didn't want a bar of him.

I tried to get her to come home, even went down to Melbourne to convince her in person, but the answer was still no.

I wish I'd known Kaye was sick. I'd have had another go at bringing her back so I could've taken care of her. And you. But I was working in Europe at the time.

Too late when I got back. I tried child services, but they didn't think I was an appropriate guardian for you, and they said you were nicely settled where you were anyway. Too much trauma to bring you away to the country to a stranger.

I hope they were right and you were fine, but it's too late to do anything about it now. Maybe it will help you know that someone wanted you.

Now there's no one left but me, and I'm eaten alive with cancer. That'd because of my time in Changi.

I wish I'd known you.

And I hope you take care, find your father, and make a good life for yourself. I'll be watching over you from where ever I end up.

James.

Finn wiped her eyes on the sleeve of her fleece and rummaged in her pockets for a tissue.

Something inside her, perhaps her frozen heart, cracked.

Her life was not the same as it'd seemed before reading the letter.

Child services were wrong.

It would've been infinitely better to grow up out here with someone who loved her for more than the foster care money.

Unforgivable to have kept this from her. To have wilfully denied her the knowledge, let alone the choice.

She dropped the letter on the table, seeming to look through a long, dark tunnel at it. Feeling twitchy, and as her pulse increased, and she heard the blood pounding in her ears.

She wanted to find the do-gooder who'd thought she was better where she was and rip their bloody arms off.

Her hands shook as she clenched them, needing to find an axe and a large tree to take her aggression out on.

Neither of which was immediately available to her.

Thwarted, she went outside, planted her feet and roared.

Muscles straining as she leaned in, screaming.

Cursing at whoever the stupid knows better than you public servant was, shouting "I'll bloody kill you," and hacking at the nearby bushes with her bare hands.

Until she collapsed, sobbing to the ground.

Kneeling in wretched misery, she decided to keep the house.

No one was going to keep her from the place she belonged ever again.

"You right Darl?" Archie asked.

She started laughing.

Almost as hysterically as she'd been screaming, tears leaking from her eyes.

Typical of her life in general - a dead person checking in on her welfare.

"Nothing a beer and a pizza wouldn't cure."

"Pizza? What's pizza?"

"Ah, it's kind of like a cheese toastie, only different."

The evening chill was drawing in, and she went back into the kitchen to warm herself by the stove.

Archie followed.

A hot Romano pizza from the pizzeria at the end of her Richmond street would've hit the spot perfectly. But she wasn't sure where the closest pizza place to the cottage was, let alone how far it would deliver.

And by the time it arrived, it would've been cold and greasy, and not appealing at all.

She had ham, cheese and tomato, as well as bread, butter and a frying pan. Not exactly the pizza she hoped for, but it would do.

Nor did she have beer, but did have wine.

So toastie with wine it was.

Archie looked on with interest as she put the sandwich together and fried it up.

"So, how did you end up here in the house?" Finn asked.

"I'm not sure exactly. It was Ma's birthday, and I'd been thinking about her. Someone triggered a land mine, and I went flying. Landed in a crater and I was lying in the mud and filth, looking up at the blue sky, wishing I was home."

He lifted his right hand and rubbed his right eye.

"I desperately wanted to see her, just one more time. And then..." he shrugged his shoulders, "somehow I was here."

Finn didn't know what to say, just nodded and flipped her sandwich onto a plate and cut it in half.

"Ma was standing by the sink over there, drinking a cup of tea. She turned around and saw me, dropped the cup and fainted."

Finn smothered a smile in her sandwich.

Not that it wasn't tragic, but she was imagining the movie version. Dropping the cup would be the comic relief to dissipate the tension.

Archie sighed. "It was the first and only time she saw me, but I was still here when she died. I thought I'd go with her, but..." He shrugged his shoulders again. "And then I thought I'd go with Edith, and then James."

Archie leaned in her direction, as though attempting to nudge her with his shoulder, "and now there's you."

He sighed, "I've about given up. Maybe there's no such place as heaven or hell. God knows I deserve to go to hell, but this... this is... torture."

Finn smiled tightly, and dropping the last of her sandwich, opened the wine and sloshed some into a glass before draining it in almost one swallow.

She poured another glass. "I don't believe in heaven or hell or any other kind of place you go when you die. The idea of this life and then my eternal reward makes me sick. I hope this one life is all there is."

"And there you were just moments ago, telling me God's own truth!"

"I thought you'd be religious, and it'd make you feel better."

Archie snorted, "is your life so bad?"

Finn snorted, "was that you outside asking me if I was okay?"

"Tell me about it?"

Finn grabbed a tissue and wiped her mouth, then turned it over, folded it up and blew her nose before dropping it on the plate with the remains of her sandwich.

"I don't know where to start."

He rested an elbow a millimetre above the table, "how about what happened to make you my little infidel?" he said.

"Watch it," she waved a finger at him, "it's more like your big infidel."

And then she sighed. Reached for the letter, swept the jewellery, wrapped package and wreckage of dinner aside with her arm and spread the pages out, side by side, on the table.

"Everything I thought I knew about my life is a lie." She jabbed the letter with a finger, "that's pretty much what it says here."

Archie didn't say or do anything, and until he blinked, she thought maybe he was buffering like a show viewed on her laptop.

"I grew up thinking Mum'd been abandoned by her people, but it turns out her pig-headedness is to blame. All that bloody time I thought I was alone..."

Finn swallowed.

"All that bloody time, I thought I was alone and unloved, but I wasn't."

She hit the table with a fist, "first Mum lied to me, then Child Services lied to me, then all those goddamned fff... foster parents."

Closing her eyes, she looked up at the ceiling and took a shaky breath, "my life has been horrific enough without going to hell on top of that as well. And as for heaven, that would just be a mockery. When the time comes, I just want it to be over."

Archie wiped his nose on his sleeve, "we're like a matched set of bookends."

She raised an eyebrow.

"You don't know what bookends are?"

She snorted, "of course I do, but I'm don't know what you mean."

"You know the kind of thing, a novelty pair. On one side, I abandoned my family, and on the other, yours abandoned you."

She gasped and scrunched up her face.

He turned away.

"Actually," she said yawning, "not entirely accurate, but a fair assessment. But now we two lost souls have found each other, so perhaps there's hope for us both after all."

She yawned again, "I'm knackered."

"Go to bed. Use the proper bed, not that thing on the floor."

Finn grinned, "I'm not sure of the propriety of sleeping in your bed."

"Hasn't been my bed for decades."

"Then what about the other time?"

"Dunno," he reached a hand out to pass through her arm and both of them shuddered, "some kind of special confluence of events."

She grinned and drained the last of the wine, "right then, I'm off to bed."

It was a kind of relief to drag the sleeping bag into the bed.

Monday dawned a little too early and a little too bright.

As Finn took her resolution to move permanently into the cottage out into the cold to use her camp toilet, she doubted her ability to get by until she installed an indoor toilet.

She didn't mind the idea of not bathing terribly much, but after a few days, a modern population of peers might not be so forgiving - there was a limit to the intensity of aroma you could cover with deodorant and perfume sprays.

And maybe it was just the drinking, but she really needed a hot shower.

Back inside, she got the stove going again, and put some water on for coffee and a sponge bath.

Not a hot shower, but it would have to do.

Then decanted more tank water and topped it up with water purifying tablets.

The thought of doing that every day was a drama, and she wondered how long it'd take to get the plumbing and electricity done.

Finn had a rough idea of the cost of some of it (a lot). She'd some savings, and her inheritance, though she wasn't expecting much. Put all together, and what could she do?

While she waited for the water to boil, she cleaned the table, put the letter back into the envelope, swept the jewellery into it, but paused at the paper-wrapped package.

She unravelled it to find a pin inside. Something like feathers? She scrubbed it with the pad of her thumb. Were they leaves? She looked through the window at the tree outside - oak leaves?

She glanced at the stained paper, and then looked again, some kind of certificate, again in copperplate.

It was creased as if someone had unfolded it, read it and refolded it hundreds of times. Some kind of fluid, perhaps tears, had made the ink run, and it was difficult to decipher.

Something... Archibald George Webb was mentioned in a Despatch from... dated thirtieth November 1915 for gallant and distinguished services... command from the King... high appreciation of services rendered.

Was the feather/leaf thing a medal?

"Archie," she called, "Archie? Come quick, I think you got a medal!"

No response.

"Archie?"

Which, oddly, reminded her of the pictures in the locket, so she took it out of the envelope to ask Archie about it later.

Coffee made, body bathed, she was ready for the day.

All dressed up, but nowhere to go.

Wanting to visit Mel but not wanting to be clingy with the only friend she had in town.

It wasn't as if Mel was exactly a friend yet, but the woman was someone Finn really liked. And her friends weren't bad either.

In her journey from foster home to foster home and school to school, Finn'd learned the first friend was the hardest, but the most critical. First friends needed nurturing.

On the other hand, Mel would probably know someone who could upgrade the house. Someone who knew about life in the country and would get the right kind of equipment she'd need.

She tried calling Archie again, but it seemed he'd more important ghost things to do.

What things she didn't know, but hoped they didn't involve moving on just when she was getting to know him.

She almost laughed as she considered her second local friend was a dead one (though technically, he'd been the first).

She drove into town.

Finn started at the bakery, with a rich, meaty pie for breakfast and a latte, sitting at a table outside to watch the town crawl into life.

Which was where Mel found her, "my goodness you're here early! I wasn't expecting you today at all."

"Oh, hello. I wasn't planning to come in, but I've decided to stay here, and was hoping you could recommend a registered builder to look at the house."

Mel groaned theatrically, "let me get a coffee; I'm cactus 'til I've got a second one and organised my thoughts."

Before too long, she was back with a large beverage and a tiny slice of some grainy thing that looked healthy. "Now, tell me everything," she said.

Mel nibbled the slice as Finn told her about the letter and her thoughts about it.

"Well, I get why you'd feel that way, but living in the country isn't for everyone. I said I'd have some work for you, but it isn't regular and I doubt it'd be enough to support you."

Finn grinned, "trying to back out now?"

"Nah, not at all," Mel put a hand on her heart, "just playing the Devil's advocate."

"One of the temp jobs I did for a while was updating documents and databases overnight, ready for the next day. If I can get the internet connected, with a reliably fast speed and minimal drop-off, I could do the same for anyone in the world."

"That sounds tedious, yet I know there have been times I'd have found a service like that useful. What sorts of records were you given for that?"

"Voice recordings, scribbled notes, pretty much everything. At least if I set up at home, I wouldn't have to go to anyone else's workplace. Or do the actual work during the actual night!"

"That's ingenious. Do you have a cash cushion in case it takes a while to establish reliable customers?"

"Probably not enough if I'm going to do my house up at the same time."

"Oh yeah," Mel tapped the edge of her phone against her lip, "I reckon Kitto or Hayden might have a gap in their schedule." She tapped her phone a couple of times, "I'm just calling now."

Finn idly picked a couple of crumbs from Mel's plate as she watched a blonde guy stride up the street. Like Archie, his muscles came from work, not exercise, though once he hurt himself, he'd probably go to seed quickly.

As she was idly wondering what he'd be like in bed, he pulled his phone from the breast pocket of his shirt and grinned as he put it back.

He walked up to their table, and in a Lurch-like tone, said, "you rang."

Mel jumped, then laughed, "Kitto! You startled me. "Finn," she pointed, "needs a registered builder to do some work at the old Webb house."

"Not the haunted how—" he said, stopping abruptly as Mel uncrossed and recrossed her legs, kicking him in the shin as she nodded her head across at Finn.

"The Webb house up on the hill?" he looked at Finn for confirmation.

"That's the one."

"It's been a while since anyone lived there. There's probably a lot that needs to be done."

Finn smiled, "there is a lot, but the main thing is an indoor bathroom along with the plumbing and electric to go with it."

"Hold on," he said, "I'll get a coffee and we can talk about it."

"Then my work here is done," Mel said, standing up. "I'm off." She took a couple of steps toward her office. "Oh, Finn, could you drop by the office on the way back?"

"Sure thing boss."

As Kitto arrived back with his coffee, Mel waved a hand dismissively and walked away.

"So," said Kitto, "what are you looking for?"

"Why did you call it the haunted house?"

"Oh, it was just a joke."

"I'm not worried about the house being haunted. I just want to know how it became a joke."

"Ah, well, okay.

"My grandparents told me that the old lady who lived there said she'd turned around and seen her son who was away in the war. And the next thing, there's a telegram from the War Office."

Kitto took a gulp of coffee and leaned in a little closer, lowering his voice, "they say she went a bit nuts after that. Her hair turned white, and she wandered around town in her dressing gown talking to herself. Until they sent her away to some place where they could take care of her."

He leaned back, "I expect it was the grief, and with no psychologists or whatever to help, she just got worse."

"That's tragic! What happened to her kids?" Finn asked.

He shrugged his shoulders, "no idea. That kind of stuff doesn't usually end up part of the legend. The Webb family was one of the town's founding families, so I imagine some relative or other took them in."

Which explained a lot, at least from James' perspective. If they'd sent him to live with someone he knew, he'd be horrified Finn was sent to strangers.

"I see. I assumed that James'd lived in the house but not got round to modernising it."

"I suppose that's another story. Look, we just had a job cancelled - Melbourne couple getting divorced of all things. Why don't I come out now and take a quick look around."

"Sure, that'd be great."

12

When Finn got back to the cottage, Kitto was already there, walking around the house taking notes on his phone.

"It's in better condition than I expected," he said, "let's take a look inside."

She opened the door, and he walked in.

"This is incredible! It's like time stood still."

"I'd noticed."

Kitto walked through the house, banging on the walls and stamping on the floors.

Archie arrived to see what was happening, and she winced when Kitto walked through him to enter the kitchen.

At any rate, it certainly looked like Kitto couldn't see Archie. Though whether anyone else could remained to be seen.

Knowing the house was in fact haunted, but Kitto couldn't see it made her smile a little.

He reverently touched the kitchen cupboards, "you don't see workmanship like that these days."

Archie looked smug.

Kitto walked through to the lean-to and checked out the water tanks.

"What exactly were you thinking of doing?"

"Just converting the lean-to into a bathroom/laundry, and maybe making the kitchen bigger. Something like a couple of metres extra across the back. Indoor plumbing and electricity."

"Okay," he said, "that's enough work to require a standard contract. There might be asbestos, so I'll need to get that checked and maybe someone to remove it.

"Otherwise, the biggest problem is the regs, but we can plan around that.

"Mains water and sewerage don't come past here, so you'll need to upgrade the tanks with a filtration and treatment system, and fix up the drainage to a septic system.

"Electricity'll be expensive because you're a ways out of town. Installing a pole and connecting it to the house is going to be ten to fifteen thousand plus wires. But you're on a hill with plenty of sunlight and wind, so you might be better to install solar panels and a battery and they'll cost about twenty.

"We'll need planning and building permits, but we'll keep it within the bounds of an online app so you won't need to go through the committee."

"Sounds complicated. And expensive."

He did some sums on his phone, "well, depending on how..." he frowned at her, "fussy you are, it'll cost anywhere between fifty grand and a hundred. Plus, potentially, whatever the electricity company charges to bring the wires out."

Finn sucked in her breath. Fifty thousand dollars was a lot of money. She looked up, trying to work out where she could get it from. Would she be able to get a loan?

Kitto noticed her anxiety, "I know it sounds a lot, but you could be eligible for a grant from Council. And if we get going at the right time, we could get some trade school apprentices in for work experience."

"Oh no, it's not that. Though less money going out is better, but I was hoping to get it done without having to get a loan."

"I understand," he thought for a moment. "Technically, you can't live here, though it's not like you have to ask anyone for permission. We could do it bit by bit as you get the money, but if we find something that needs doing, I can't ignore it. So that being the case, what's the most urgent thing you need?"

"Indoor toilet. No! Wait. Electricity."

"Right," he added the cost up on his phone. "Say one switch, one light, and one double socket for each of the five rooms, a fuse box, a couple of smoke detectors, and lights at the back and front. About four grand. Plus at least twenty to run the electricity to the house."

Finn winced. Twenty-five thousand might as well be twenty-five million.

Kitto patted her back, "as a temporary option, you could buy a petrol or diesel generator for a couple of grand, though it might not do the whole house."

Finn sighed, "I feel like the universe is against me."

"Nah, it's not that bad," Kitto said, but she was looking past him, talking to Archie.

Whose spirits seemed to have decreased with the numbers Kitto was quoting. Fifty thousand dollars must seem like an overwhelming amount of money to him; a loaf of bread probably cost something like five pence or less when he left Australia.

"I wish I could help you," he said.

Finn rubbed her temples. Clearly, she had some thinking to do. "I don't know much about this kind of thing, but do you think you could work up a plan and an estimate? Maybe tell me what you recommend in terms of getting it done."

Kitto grinned, "I'd normally expect a deposit, but as you're one of Mel's friends, I'll lay out a quick and dirty for you. And I'll check out the grant situation, and getting the apprentices in too."

"Would you? That's wonderful. Thank you so much!"

"Maybe you could put in a good word with Mel for me then?"

"Of course! That's the least I could do."

13

After Kitto left, she made herself another cup of coffee and watched the clouds scud across the sky as she drank it.

Archie appeared next to her, "are you okay?"

Finn shrugged, "I'm not sure. Near where I live there's a house that's had a piece of chipboard in a window for years, and I've always wondered why they don't just fix it."

She turned to look at him, "owning a house is more expensive and complicated than I'd imagined."

"I could say the same for life in general. Or death, for that matter."

Finn sob-snorted, "I don't know what to do."

"I think the house is perfectly serviceable as it is," Archie grinned.

"It's a little harder for me... Oh, I never asked about bin day."

He looked at her quizzically.

"Never mind," she said, "it's another one of those modern conveniences. It was easier in your day; no plastics or non-recyclables to dispose of."

She sipped her coffee, her mind resisting the idea of selling the jewellery she'd just got.

Mel said there was work.

Damn.

She was supposed to see Mel before she left town. Finn rifled through the papers Mel'd given her, looking for a business card or phone number, but there wasn't anything there.

She'd no option but to drive back to town.

The half-hour drive was charming, but the thought of money wasted on the trip made her feel even more poverty-stricken.

She needed to get more organised, not be wasting time or money driving into town more often than she needed to.

At which point, she wondered whether she had enough fuel to get back.

You needed a different kind of organised for life in the country.

Back in town, with a full tank of petrol, Finn visited Mel at her office.

"You took a while," Mel said, "I didn't think Kitto was that entertaining?"

"Um, no. Yes. No. We went to the cottage to see what needs doing and how much it might cost."

Mel grabbed a fat file and gestured her into the meeting room, "and?"

"At best, fifty thousand. At worse, more than one hundred thousand dollars."

"Well, that's a pretty good price for what needs doing, so what's with the sad face?"

Finn pulled out a chair and flopped into it, "it just seems like a lot of money right now," she took a deep breath and sighed, "I'll have to apply for a loan and without a decent employment record, I doubt I'll get one."

Mel snorted, "still want the cottage then?"

"Absolutely! I may just need to get used to living like a pioneer. Wait," she looked at Mel, "why didn't Kitto tell me I could get a solar generator?"

Mel shrugged, "maybe there's something about the installation? Or you need to hook it up to mains power to charge?"

"Don't know. I'll need to do some more research. Anyway, what was it you wanted?"

Mel shuffled through the papers in the file and pulled out a form. "If you're sure you want to keep the property, here's the transfer of land papers to be signed."

"Ah right, of course."

The lawyer pushed the papers and a pen towards Finn, who signed them where Mel pointed.

"I'll pay the fee and lodge the forms, and in a week or two, you'll be the proud owner of a house that needs at least fifty thousand dollars' worth of work done. Once the transfer's complete, I can wind up the estate and transfer the remaining funds to your account."

"Great, thanks very much."

"Don't you want to know how much money we're talking about?"

"I wouldn't have thought much, James was just an old guy on a pension."

"Why would you say that?"

"He hasn't upgraded the cottage, so he can't have had any money."

"He didn't live in it."

"What?"

Mel let her digest the information for a moment. "His mother left him her house when she died, and he sold it when he moved into palliative care."

"So the cottage was only ever owned by Archie? Well, not owned, but lived in?"

She shuffled through the file again, "yes, that's right. They gave him a piece of the old farm when he got engaged, and he built the house for his fiancé."

Finn gaped. Just as she'd thought.

Mel pulled out a piece of paper and pushed it across the table for Finn to see, but she didn't look at it immediately.

"Who was his fiancé?"

"Don't know. I think she moved to the city."

"Burnley Agricultural College?"

"Couldn't say. Why did you ask?"

"Edna Walling."

Mel raised an eyebrow, clearly not understanding.

"Burnley Agricultural College was the first Australian college to accept women. After the war, a lot of single women enrolled and went on to become landscapers."

Mel nodded, not really interested, and jiggled the paper.

Finn looked at it and let out a bark of laughter. "I've never seen that much money. Where did it all come from?"

"Hmmm. Where to start," Mel said, tapping her fingers together. "When your mother left town, James asked my grandfather to open a trust. Put a couple of hundred down and made regular payments. Same when he heard about you. When Kaye was sick, she refused to touch the money, and when she died, he transferred the balance into your trust."

Finn's eyes watered as Mel continued, "he made a bit of money while he was overseas, but he lived a pretty frugal life. Never got married; never met the right girl he used to say."

Mel grabbed a box of tissues from a shelf behind her and slid it across the table, "now and again someone would ask him for help, and he'd buy a house or a tractor or something and rent it out to them at a discounted price.

"And when he found out he was dying, he started liquidating his assets, so when we finally found you, you wouldn't have to do anything except decide what to do with the money."

Finn blew her nose. "Then why leave me the cottage?"

Mel looked steadily at her then sighed, looking up at the law books that surrounded her, "by the time it went up on the market, it was well established as a haunted house and it just didn't sell."

Finn leaned over the look at the numbers on the bottom of the bank statement again.

Just to check again, she hadn't been mistaken.

"And how did it come by that reputation?"

Mel sighed again, "the way I heard it, Old Mrs Webb was convinced the ghost of Archie lived there. She used to visit him every day to keep the house clean and tidy for him, and when it needed something doing, she'd badger James to take care of it.

"So many young men died during the first world war, and I think the town wanted to believe they were still here."

Mel scrubbed her face with both hands, "anyway, he promised her he'd take care of the house, and he did. Before he died, he went out there with someone to make sure the maintenance was up to date, and it was secure."

"Do you think James saw Archie there as well?"

"Why, have you seen him?"

"Of course not. I don't believe in ghosts."

"Of course not," Mel smiled, "I dare same James didn't believe in ghosts either."

It was Finn's turn to sigh. "I guess I don't need to worry about the cost of doing up the house anymore."

"Does that change anything for you?"

Finn grinned, "I want to go back to Melbourne to throw out all my stuff so I can buy fresh furniture and bits and bobs to come back with. And I want to do it immediately."

"As a technicality, if you give me your bank account details, I could transfer the bulk of the money to you today as the first instalment. Actually, now that we've found you, I should at least transfer the trust fund to you."

Finn sucked in a breath, then slowly let it out. "I'm not sure that's wise. Better to give me some time to think about what to do with it all first."

15

With so much to think about, Finn barely noticed the drive home.

The biggest question was whether James knew Archie was at the cottage?

Had he watched his brother remain young as he grew old?

What was the poem they read at the Anzac Day dawn services?

They shall grow not old, as we that are left grow old:
Age shall not weary them, nor the years condemn.
At the going down of the sun and in the morning
We will remember them.

Finn sighed and poured herself a glass of wine.

Archie joined her in the kitchen. "Do you always sigh this much?"

She took a sip and shrugged, "probably. I've always found rather a lot to sigh about."

"No need for sighing now."

"Oh, I just wanted to check something with you," she set the wine down and picked up the locket, pointing at the mystery man, "is this James?"

Archie leaned over to look, "not that I knew him because he was a baby when I left, but it's Ma's locket so probably."

She looked at it again, "he seems... I don't know, fun. I feel like I'd have liked him."

Archie shrugged as Finn picked up her wine again. Folding her left arm across her chest, and holding the glass up to her chin in her right, "did James see you? Or talk to you?"

"He used to come to the house, but I couldn't say for sure he ever saw me. Not like you do. He certainly did a lot of talking, but I feel it was more of a thinking out loud kind of thing."

"What about your mother? I think you said she saw you once?"

"Same thing, she talked a lot, but not a conversation as such. You're the first person who's heard me talk back. I expect that's why I can't seem to shut up!"

"Oh. I wonder if it's because I nearly died when I was a child?"

"Goodness, that's strange and interesting. What happened?"

"Dunno. Don't remember. Woke up in hospital and never got a proper explanation from my mother. Though I don't suppose she expected to die so young."

"Why did you ask?"

"Oh," she took a sip of wine, "just that Mel, the lawyer, said James promised to take care of this house because your mother thought you were still here. So, I wondered if they knew for sure."

He shrugged.

"But after that thing this morning, I wondered if you minded me doing some upgrades around here."

"Why would I mind? It's your house now."

"I don't know, I was just worried you'd go all poltergeist on me?"

"Poltergeist? What's poltergeist?" He looked as concerned as if she'd threatened him with tuberculosis, so Finn grinned.

"A poltergeist is the kind of ghost who's generally upset and throws things about."

"I'm definitely not one of those," he pushed his hand through the wine bottle she'd left on the table, "but there's still time."

Finn laughed and moved the bottle towards the centre of the table.

"What about your fiancé?"

"Ahhh. The lovely Lillian... No. She certainly didn't visit the house while I was alive, so I can't imagine why she might have visited after I'd gone."

"Because you were gone. And this was the house you built her.

"Hey, wait a minute," Finn put her glass on the table and rummaged about trying to find the jewellery.

"Was this your ring?" she asked as she opened up the box.

He put a finger out to touch it, before pulling it away, "your ring now dear."

"Would you mind telling me about it?"

He sighed. "The tradition at the time was birthstones, and Lillian was born in May, thus the emerald. Diamonds - the unbreakable stone represented our unbreakable bond."

He blurred around the edges. "Funny when you think about it, that I came to mother when I died, and not Lillian. I wonder why she gave the ring back."

"Tell me her name and I'll find her."

But he dissolved from view.

Finn panicked. Had he gone for good?

Then gulped more wine.

Whether he returned or not, he'd given her permission to upgrade the building.

Not as if she needed it, because Archie was dead. And she didn't really believe ghosts could harm you.

16

Finn made herself another toastie for a late lunch/early dinner, but found the fire had gone out because she'd forgotten to bank it again.

Cursing, she re-laid and relit it, putting a kettle full of water on the stove to boil in case the fire went out shortly after.

In the meantime, she tidied up the kitchen again and dragged a pot of instant noodles out of her camping box to eat.

As she slurped the noodles, she thought about what she'd learned in the last few days.

Aside from being richer than she'd ever imagined.

She'd found her family and learned where she'd come from. Her homecoming brought meaning to her childhood suffering and offered a new direction.

Though she'd no idea where this new direction was heading.

Best of all, after finding her place, she'd grown a root, with new friends and a new community.

There was nothing to keep her in Melbourne. She could almost just not go back.

Aside from having to move all her things out and close out the lease so she could stop paying rent.

Her thoughts drifted to modern conveniences. It was nice having the heating come on automatically on frosty mornings. And flicking a switch to flood a room with light. The coffee maker, hot and cold running water.

The size of the cottage was fine; a bedroom and slightly smaller study. Perhaps open up the kitchen wall, so the lounge became part of a larger combined room.

Or turn the slightly larger lounge into a study and combine the smaller bedroom with the kitchen?

Get a surveyor out to see where the land started and stopped and maybe move the driveway, so the approach to the house gave the bedroom more privacy.

Perhaps a room for storage, and maybe another for guests to stay. Though who was going to come out to visit was a mystery.

With money no object, she could do whatever she wanted.

Even install concrete underground water tanks and sit the cottage on top.

And even with more or less limitless money, she absolutely, positively, definitely didn't want to get rid of the cottage.

Or the wood stove in the kitchen.

She checked the time on her phone and decided she'd have time to call Kitto before it got too late.

Five months later, Finn'd scattered her mother's ashes safely in the ocean, and was on her way back In a new car, with a puppy fixed securely in the back seat, the drive along a fenced road hinting at what was to come.

She triggered the electric gates, and once she'd driven through, triggered the closure.

The realigned drive lined with oak saplings hinted at the magnificence of what the newly planted garden would become.

Perfection.

The cottage was fresh with white paint, deep blue tin sheets on the roof, and colonial windows gleaming in the warm sunshine.

She let the dog loose and paused nervously before opening the door.

The first thing she saw was Archie leaning against the kitchen bench.

"Welcome home," he said.

THE END

This book cites two poems written during, and about the First World War.

Wilfred Owen wrote "Dulce et Decorum est" in 1917 (referenced p. 20),

The original line *Dulce et decorum est pro patria mori* comes from Horace's "Odes" (III.2.13) and is literally translated as "It is sweet and fitting to die for the homeland."

As time passed, they commonly used this sentiment for recruitment and propaganda purposes.

Owen's poem "Dulce et Decorum est" describes the appalling nature of war and criticised Horace's sentiment, calling it "The old lie."

Owen died in action in 1918, just a week short of Armistice Day.

His poetry was and published posthumously as *Poems of Wilfred Owen* in 1920.

The second poem, referenced on p. 89, is "For the Fallen," by Laurence Binyon.

Binyon wrote it in 1914, in mourning for the deaths following the British Expeditionary Force's defeat at the Battle of Mons and the subsequent evacuation.

The "Ode of Remembrance," as read at many commemorative services, particularly ANZAC dawn services, comes from the fourth stanza of "For the Fallen," and never fails to send a chill down my spine.

Anzac Day commemorates the Gallipoli dawn landing on April 25, 1915.

The original plan was for the Australian and New Zealand Army Corps (ANZACs) to capture the peninsular to open the Dardanelles to the allied navies.

However, the Turkish opposition was stronger than expected, and the attack resulted in an eight-month stalemate.

Later that year, they evacuated the soldiers, leaving over eight thousand dead.

The first dawn commemoration took place in 1916, but as time passed, and Australia took part in more wars, the day serves as a commemoration for all who died in military and peacekeeping campaigns.

ABOUT THE AUTHOR

Alexandria Blaelock writes stories, some of them for *Ellery Queen's Mystery Magazine* and *Pulphouse Fiction Magazine*.

She's also written five self-help books applying business techniques to personal matters like getting dressed, cleaning house, and feeding your friends.

Discover more at www.alexandriablaelock.com.

… you might also like The Histories of Hayward Hall.

Meet Morag Clementine. The new housekeeper at historic Hayward Hall.

Her practical and capable attitude usually keeps her out of trouble. Above all, her no-nonsense, get it done approach. And her get in the middle of the scrum outlook. Just as well, because Hayward Hall needs someone like her.

In this genre-spanning collection of original stories, Morag finds herself ensnared in the History of Hayward Hall…

- The Space-Time Paradox – in which we meet our plucky heroine on her first day at work.
- Love in the Past Tense – she crash lands in 1905.
- The Mystery of the Master Suite – she disappears in mysterious circumstances.
- The Ghost Detectors – she's visited by a paranormal investigator in an alternate dimension.
- Special Relativity in Space – she returns to her own time.

No ordinary housekeeper, can Morag save the house, one century at a time?